A STORMY NIGHT ON TANGLEWELD ISLAND

by Hilary Horder Hippely

illustrated by Barbara Upton

For my son, Luke,
and for our friend and teacher,
Susan Ann Holmberg
H.H.H.

For my parents, Howard and Jean
B.U.

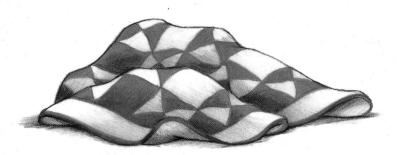

First published in the US in 1998 by
Dutton Children's Books,
a member of Penguin Putnam Inc

First published in Great Britain in 1999 by
Macdonald Young Books
an imprint of Wayland Publishers Ltd
61 Western Road
Hove
BN3 1JD

ISBN: 0 7500 2699 5
ISBN: 0 7500 2700 2 (pb)

Printed in Hong Kong

British Library in Publication Data available

One dark autumn night
the full moon was hiding;
I heard the wind moan
and saw the sea rising.

"It's a storm," I told Teddy
and tucked him in tight.
"That noisy old thunder
might rumble all night.

"But with our snuggly blanket
there's nothing to fear;
at least we're not out
with the birds and the deer."

I was growing quite sleepy
    and closing my eyes,
when I saw Teddy jump up
    and to my surprise

he reached for his coat –
    "Someone's calling," he said.
"We won't be much help
    if we stay here in bed!"

So I snatched up our blanket
and quick as can be
we crept down the stairs
and ran to the sea.

The rowing boat bobbed
by the creaky old docks;
I climbed in with Ted
and we rowed past the rocks.

Then waves threw us high
and crashed us down low,
we almost lost track
of which way to go.

The island grew closer.
  "Row hard," I told Ted.
"It's getting much bigger –
  it's just up ahead!"

We took a deep breath
  and stepped on to the sand,
clutching our blanket
  and each other's hand.

The beach seemed quite empty
  with no one to see.
But who had been calling
  to Teddy and me?

We heard a few sniffles,
    then somebody sneezed,
and a tearful old rabbit
    hopped out from the trees.

We ran to his side
    as he pointed his paw.
Our eyes filled with tears
    at the sad sight we saw.

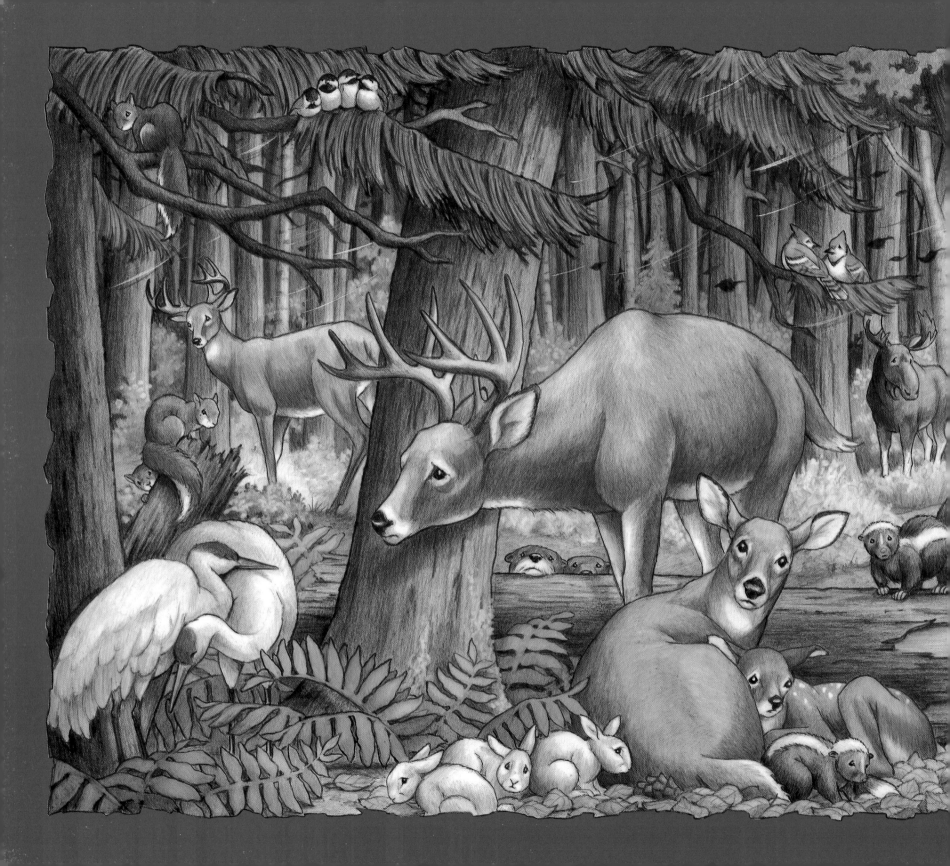

Skunks, squirrels, rabbits,
   birds, otters and deer,
were all huddled together
   and shaking with fear.

"We're scared," Rabbit said,
   "to be out in this storm.
We should all stay together –
   cosy and warm.

"But our nests and our burrows
   and caves are too small.
We can't find a home
   the right size for us all."

They sobbed and they cried
   and they all howled together.
How could they keep dry
   in this terrible weather?

"Our blanket is warm,"
   I said, waving it high.
"It helps us feel brave.
   So please, please don't cry."

"But first we need shelter
   from this dark, stormy sky.
We need to build something
   to keep us all dry."

"Let me help," said Eagle.
"I'm an excellent scout.
I'll find the best sticks
and twigs lying about."

"I'll fetch them," cried Moose.
"Let me help," added Deer.
"I'll haul up some driftwood —
the beach is so near."

"We'll need seashells and weed,"
    Otter cried to his friends,
as the stags picked up wood
    with their horns' jagged ends.

Bear brought huge boulders.
    and piled them up high –
building up a great fireplace
    towards the dark sky.

Deer carried branches;
    birds flew with weed;
the rabbits brought twigs –
    we had all we could need.

"Rumble! Boom!" crashed the thunder,
    but now no one cared;
with so much to work on
    how could we be scared?

With Teddy arranging
 the things that we'd brought,
soon rising before us
 stood Tangleweed Fort!

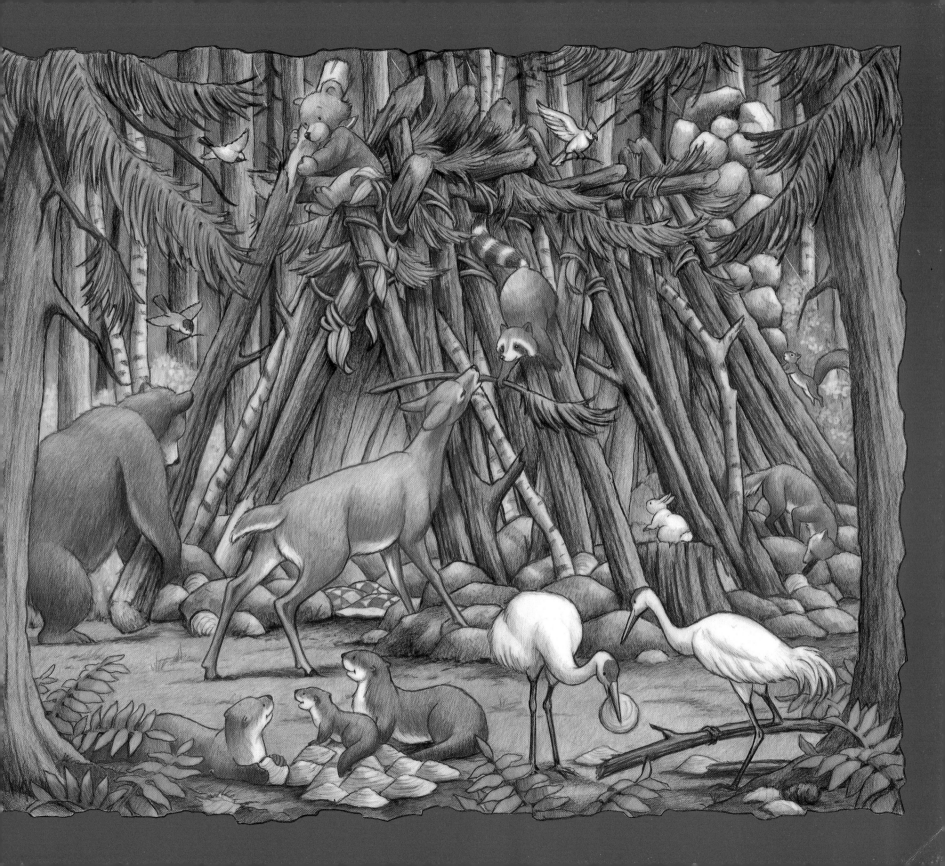

For a moment we stood
    in that terrible weather,
amazed by the home
    we had all built together.

Then Moose led a cheer –
    "Hip hooray!" we all cried,
and hurried to fill up
    the warm space inside.

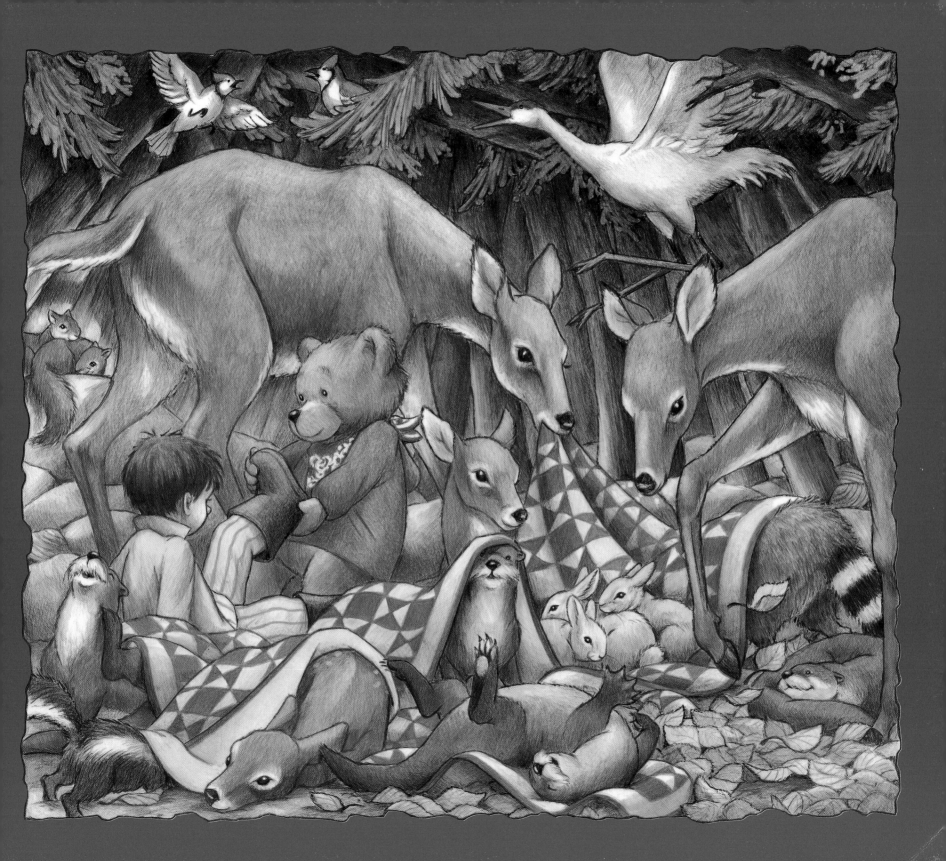

"Now a story," said Rabbit.
   "It's time for a tale."
He was clearing his throat
   when we heard a sad wail.

A poor baby otter
   cried out to us all:
"I'm still cold! No one's sharing!
   This blanket's too small!"

"Don't worry!" cried Teddy.
  "You'll soon be quite warm;
wrapped up in my scarf,
    away from the storm!"

"Now I'm cosy," sighed Otter.
"I really can't grumble."
But everyone laughed
at his stomach's loud rumble.

So Otter's dear grannie
with a wink of her eye,
baked a marvellous
walnut and blackberry pie.

Before long we got sleepy
    by that warm fireside,
while the wind moaned and howled
    and the rain poured outside.

Soon an eagle was yawning
    high up in a tree;
and the whole clan all snored
    except Teddy and me.

"Sleep tight," I told Ted,
    as I gave him a hug.
"We'll stay here till morning –
    safe, warm and snug."

But the storm must have broken
    as we both lay there dreaming.
When we opened our eyes,
    the full moon was gleaming.

We tiptoed away
    so our friends wouldn't wake,
and we rowed the dark sea —
    now as still as a lake.

We woke in the morning,
    our room full of light,
but we know where to go
    the next dark, stormy night!